Captain Buckleboots
on the Naughty Step

written by **Mark Sperring**

illustrated by **Tom McLaughlin**

This is Sam, and this is the naughty step.

The naughty step is right
at the bottom of the stairs. It's the place
where Sam has to sit if he ever behaves badly.

When Sam sits there,
he can't look at a book
or play with a toy.

All he can do
is think
and think
and think
about the naughty thing
he's done.

No one else in the house has
to sit on the naughty step.

When Rover is naughty,
he has to go to his basket.

When Nellie is naughty,
she has to go to her room.

And when Dad is naughty,
he has to sleep on the sofa.

So Sam **always** had the naughty step to himself, until . . .

. . . one day, with a loud creeeaak,

someone else appeared.

"Who are you?" asked Sam, looking up at a shame-faced pirate, who sat down beside him.

"I'm Captain Buckleboots," he replied. "And in case you're wondering why I'm here, I've been naughty . . .

very,

VERY

naughty."

"Oh dear," said Sam, "so have I."

Then the naughty step gave **another**

creak . . .

"Jumping jellyfish!"
cried Captain Buckleboots.
"What's he doing here?"

"Have you been naughty too?"
Sam asked the little monster,
who sat down to join them.

But before the monster could answer,
the step gave

two

more

creaks . . .

. . . and with the *swish* of a spacesuit
and the clunk of armour,
down sat an astronaut
and down sat a knight.

Suddenly the naughty step
was fuller than it had
ever been before.

So there they all sat
with nothing else to do
but **think** about
the naughty things
they'd done.

"I flew off in a **RAGE**," admitted the astronaut.

"And I was caught FIGHTING again," confessed the knight.

"And I behaved like a **LITTLE MONSTER**,"
said the little monster.

"GRRRRR!"

"How about you, Captain Buckleboots?"
asked Sam. "What did you do?"

"Oh dear, oh dear, I behaved WORSE than the
lot of you put together," blushed Captain Buckleboots.

"First I picked on a pirate smaller than me."

"That's **bad**," said the astronaut.

"Then I took something that wasn't mine."

"That's **awful**," said the knight.

"Then I buried it in a place where he'd never be able to find it."

"How **monstrous**," said the monster.

"And, worst of all, when I was asked where it was, I said I didn't know."

"Oh dear," said Sam, "you've been **VERY** naughty."

"I know," sighed Captain Buckleboots. "How will I **ever** be forgiven?"

"Well . . ." said the astronaut, "when I
get off the naughty step, I'm going to give
everyone a **big hug** and say I'm **sorry**."

"And when I get off the naughty step," said the knight, "I'm going to **promise** not to fight any more."

"And when I get off the naughty step, I'm going to be **sweet** and **lovely** and not 'GRRRRR' so much," said the monster.

Captain Buckleboots thought hard for a moment.
"But because I've behaved **SO** badly," he said, "surely I'll
need to do **something** even **MORE special** to be forgiven?"

"Well," said Sam, "you could write
a **sorry note**."

"Jumping jellyfish!"
exclaimed Captain Buckleboots.
"What a jolly good idea!"

"You can get OFF the naughty step now!" Sam's mum called from the kitchen.

"Goodbye, Sammy my lad," said Captain Buckleboots. "Now I'm off to deliver this **very important letter**. Do you think I'll be forgiven?"

"Of course," said Sam, "if you **really mean it** when you say you're sorry, you're **sure** to be forgiven."

And, **jumping jellyfish**,
Sam was right!

the naughty
step

Sam's
house

Space station

dragon valley

Dear Someone smaller than me,

This is where I buried your treasure.

Sorry, sorry, SORRY!

Best wishes,

Captain Buckleboots

P.S. If you need some help
digging it up, me and my friend
Sam would be happy to help.

monster
woods

So, at the end of a BUSY day on the naughty step, it was time for Sam to write a **Very Important Letter** of his own . . .

To mummy
I'm sorry
Love Sam x

. . . and because he **really**

REALLY meant it,
he was **sure** he'd be forgiven.

For Claire and Adi on
Howard Road – M.S.

For my nan and grandpa,
Marie and George – T.M.

PUFFIN BOOKS
Published by the Penguin Group: London, New York,
Australia, Canada, India, Ireland, New Zealand and South Africa
Penguin Books Ltd, Registered Offices:
80 Strand, London WC2R 0RL, England
puffinbooks.com
First published 2011
Text copyright © Mark Sperring, 2011
Illustrations copyright © Tom McLaughlin, 2011
Made and printed in China
ISBN: 978–0–141–32993–2
004 – 10 9 8 7 6 5 4